This is

MRS. MOON AND HER FRIENDS

Get to know Mrs. Moon and her many friends . . . and share in their adventures.

Read all 10 books
— written by Pearl Augusta Harwood

Mrs. Moon's STORY HOUR

Mrs. Moon AND HER FRIENDS

Mrs. Moon's POLLIWOGS

Mrs. Moon's PICNIC

Mrs. Moon GOES SHOPPING

Mrs. Moon's HARBOR TRIP

Mrs. Moon AND THE DARK STAIRS

Mrs. Moon's RESCUE

Mrs. Moon TAKES A DRIVE

Mrs. Moon's CEMENT HAT

You will also enjoy . . .

the Mr. Bumba books

Mr. Bumba's NEW HOME
Mr. Bumba PLANTS A GARDEN
Mr. Bumba KEEPS HOUSE
Mr. Bumba AND THE ORANGE GROVE
Mr. Bumba's NEW JOB
Mr. Bumba's A PARTY
Mr. Bumba DRAWS A KITTEN
Mr. Bumba's FOUR-LEGGED COMPANY
Mr. Bumba RIDES A BICYCLE
Mr. Bumba's TUESDAY CLUB

the Mr. & Mrs. Bumba books

A LONG VACATION for Mr. & Mrs. Bumba
THE RUMMAGE SALE and Mr. & Mrs. Bumba
A SPECIAL GUEST for Mr. & Mrs. Bumba
THE MAKE-IT ROOM of Mr. & Mrs. Bumba
A THIEF VISITS Mr. & Mrs. Bumba
A HAPPY HALLOWEEN for Mr. & Mrs. Bumba
NEW YEAR'S DAY with Mr. & Mrs. Bumba
THE CARNIVAL with Mr. & Mrs. Bumba
CLIMBING A MOUNTAIN with Mr. & Mrs. Bumba
THE VERY BIG PROBLEM of Mr. & Mrs. Bumba

MRS. MOON
AND
HER FRIENDS

by **Pearl Augusta Harwood**

pictures by **George Overlie**

Lerner Publications Company
Minneapolis, Minnesota

Copyright © 1967 by Lerner Publications Company

All rights reserved. International copyright secured.
Manufactured in the United States of America. Pub-
lished simultaneously in Canada by J. M. Dent &
Sons Ltd., Don Mills, Ontario.

International Standard Book Number: 0-8225-0112-0
Library of Congress Catalog Card Number: 67-15688

Fourth Printing 1972

Maria was knocking on Mrs. Moon's door.

"Come in, come in!" said Mrs. Moon.
"Snow Boy and I were just hoping for some
company."

The white cat jumped from his chair. He
came to rub against Maria's leg. He purred
loudly.

"Oh, Snow Boy," said Maria. "I don't
know what to do about little Tara."

"What is the matter with little Tara?" asked Mrs. Moon.

Maria held her head down. "I laughed at her," she said. "She was trying to say a word in English. It sounded funny, and I laughed. Now she won't try to talk English at all. She just talks the talk of India."

"Oh dear," said Mrs. Moon. "Tara must learn English, or she will have a hard time at school."

They sat down to think.

"I can show lots of pictures at our next story hour," said Mrs. Moon. "We can name the things in the pictures."

There was a knock on the door. It was William, from downstairs.

"My mother sent you up these cookies for our story hour tomorrow," said William.

"Oh, how nice!" said Mrs. Moon.

"M-m-m-m!" said Maria.

"We are trying to think how to get little Tara to talk again," said Mrs. Moon.

"I laughed at her, and now she won't talk English at all," said Maria.

"She needs to see lots of new things," said Mrs. Moon.

"Oh," said William. "I know where we can show her lots and lots of new things."

"Where?" asked Maria.

William whispered something to Mrs. Moon.

"Why, what a good idea!" said Mrs. Moon. "I'll ask him this very day."

"Ask who what?" asked Maria.

Mrs. Moon smiled, and showed a dimple in each round cheek.

"You'll see, tomorrow, — maybe," she said.

The next afternoon, ten boys and girls were in Mrs. Moon's apartment. They all lived in the big house with the brownstone front.

There was William, with his two sisters and his two brothers.

There was Rebecca, with her brother Dan.

There were Tony and Maria, the Jolly
Jumpers. They wanted to be acrobats when they
grew up.

And there was little brown Tara, from
India. All the boys and girls were talking, but
Tara did not say anything at all.

"Where are the books for the story hour?" asked Rebecca. "There aren't any beside your chair."

Mrs. Moon smiled in a secret way. Her round face showed two dimples.

"I don't think I'll tell you any stories today," she said.

"Oh, oh, why not, Mrs. Moon?" they all said. "Why not?"

"Well," said Mrs. Moon, "would you like to walk up to the top floor?"

"Oh, to Captain Jack's place!" cried Dan.

"Is he going to tell the stories?" cried Maria.

"Maybe," said Mrs. Moon.

They left Snow Boy in his chair. "He is a cat who likes to stay alone," said Mrs. Moon. "He has everything he needs."

They were so quiet that Captain Jack did not hear them coming.

William knocked on the door. Then it opened.

"Well, well, what a surprise!" said big Captain Jack. He rubbed his red beard.

They all laughed. "You knew we were coming!" said William. "Didn't you?"

"Well, yes, maybe I did," said Captain Jack. "Come in, come in, to the South Sea Cove!"

The boys and girls looked around in great surprise.

"Is that the cove?" asked Tony. He pointed to a wall. The wall was all covered with a painting of ocean and land and rocks.

"That's it, that's the cove," said Captain Jack. "And here is my little grass shack."

There was a real grass shack in front of a window. The window of the room was the window for the shack.

William walked inside the shack and looked out the window. It was raining.

"There's our harbor out there," said William. "And there's your cove in here on the wall."

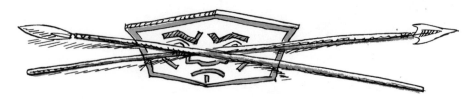

"That way, I can be in two places at once!" laughed Captain Jack.

"What is a cove?" asked Tara.

Maria looked at Mrs. Moon. "She's talking!" she whispered.

"It's a little quiet place, where the sea water runs into the land and forms a little bay," said Captain Jack.

"What's the shack FOR?" asked Maria.

"It's to make me think I'm in Tahiti," said Captain Jack. "Inside it, I have my table and my chair. I sit there and write about my travels. It will be a book, someday."

"What the dickens!" said someone inside the grass shack. William was in there, but it was not William.

William looked up at the roof of the shack. "Oh, it's your parrot!" he said. "He's up there in the middle."

"Wiki Wiki!" said the parrot, and flew out to Captain Jack's hand.

"That's his name," said Captain Jack. "In Hawaii that means 'hurry up!' "

"Did the parrot come from Hawaii?" asked Rebecca.

"Yes, a sailor owned him," said William. "He's a very smart parrot, aren't you, Wiki?"

Tara stood and looked at the parrot. She laughed out loud. She said "Wiki Wiki, Wiki Wiki, Wiki Wiki!" She ran and felt the walls.

"These walls are bamboo," said Captain Jack.

"Bamboo!" said Tara.

She ran to a starfish that was on a rock. She touched it. "What is this?" she asked.

"Starfish," said William. "It's only painted on the wall. Just like the coral rocks in the picture. And the red flowers."

The boys and girls showed Tara other things, and told her their names.

"Rocks," said Tara. "Fish. Water. Ocean. Parrot. Shack. Bamboo. Shells. Crabs." She said the names after they told her. Her face had a great big smile.

Maria was looking happy, too. "Tara is talking again!" she whispered to herself.

"Will a grass roof keep the rain out?" asked Dan.

"Yes," said Captain Jack. "See, it's put on in bunches. One bunch is over another, like shingles."

"Did you know any boys and girls who lived in grass shacks?" asked Tony.

"Oh yes, indeed," said Captain Jack. "In Tahiti, there were my good friends, Koa and Pili."

"Please tell us about them!" said William.

"Get a wiggle on!" cried the parrot, pulling Captain Jack's hair. "What the dickens!"

Mrs. Moon laughed so hard that she had to sit down on a chair. Captain Jack laughed too, and sat down in another chair. The boys and girls sat down on the floor. There were straw mats there.

"Well," said Captain Jack, "my two young friends in Tahiti, Koa and Pili, had a small canoe all their own.

"They paddled around in the lagoon, where there were no big waves.

"They were not to go outside the lagoon, where the waves were big and strong. But one day they did.

"A big wave tipped them over. They had to swim in the deep water. They swam almost back to the lagoon.

"Then Koa cried out, 'Manoa, manoa!' A shark was coming after them. She swam faster."

"Oh!" said Maria. "A shark can swim faster than people can!"

"I was in my canoe," said Captain Jack. "I went as fast as I could, to help them.

"Pili turned around in the water. He shouted at the shark. He had a knife in his hand, for he was going to try to kill the shark.

"The shark saw me coming in my canoe. I shouted, too. He was scared by all the shouting. He turned and swam out to sea.

"Koa and Pili were safe. We got their canoe back to shore. And they never went out of the lagoon again in their canoe."

"I should think not!" said Dan.

"I'm glad they got back all right," said Rebecca.

"Now I will tell you some more stories," said Captain Jack.

He told stories for one-half hour more. Then they ate the cookies that William's mother made. After that, it was time to go home.

"Thank you, thank you, Captain Jack!" said everyone.

"It was a wonderful way to spend a rainy afternoon," said Maria.

"Get a wiggle on! What the dickens!" said the parrot.

"Oh, keep quiet!" said Captain Jack. "You really are a rascal."

The parrot flew to the top of Captain Jack's head. He called, "Good-bye, good-bye, good-bye, good Wiki!"

"Good-bye, Wiki Wiki! Good-bye Captain Jack!" said the boys and girls.

Tara looked at the parrot until Captain Jack closed the door. Then she took Mrs. Moon's hand.

"I want to go there again," she said.

"Why, Tara!" said Maria. "You said — you said a lot of words together. You can talk English now!"

"Yes," said Tara. "Get a wiggle on! What the dickens! Wiki-Wiki-Wiki!"